COUNTRY · EXPLORERS ·

A Visit to

ECUADOR

by Charis Mather

BEARPORT
PUBLISHING

Minneapolis, Minnesota

T0417865

Credits

All images are courtesy of Shutterstock.com, unless otherwise specified. With thanks to Getty Images, Thinkstock Photo, and iStockphoto.

Cover – ireneuke, Jess Kraft, Dancake. 2–3 – ireneuke. 4–5 – Jess Kraft, NPeter. 6–7 – SL-Photography, Imnamlas, Gil C. 8–9 – Barna Tanko, Ecuadorpostales. 10–11 – Giuseppe Flandoli, Jess Kraft. 12–13 – Miguel Lincango, Noradoa, SL-Photography. 14–15 – Ammit Jack, FOTOGRIN, Jane Rix-Shutterstock. 16–17 – Ksenia Ragozina, robert gibson z. 18–19 – Fabian Ponce Garcia, Steve Barze. 20–21 – Ammit Jack, Gonzalo Buzonni. 22–21 – Hugo Brizard – YouGoPhoto. MarinaaaniraM.

Library of Congress Cataloging-in-Publication Data is available at www.loc.gov or upon request from the publisher.

ISBN: 979-8-88509-371-2 (hardcover)
ISBN: 979-8-88509-493-1 (paperback)
ISBN: 979-8-88509-608-9 (ebook)

© 2023 Booklife Publishing
This edition is published by arrangement with Booklife Publishing.

For more information, write to Bearport Publishing, 5357 Penn Avenue South, Minneapolis, MN 55419.

CONTENTS

COUNTRY TO COUNTRY

Which country do you live in?

A country is an area of land marked by **borders**. The people in each country have their own rules and ways of living. They may speak different languages.

Each country around the world has its own interesting things to see and do. Let's take a trip to visit a country and learn more!

Have you ever visited another country?

TODAY'S TRIP IS TO
ECUADOR!

Ecuador

NORTH AMERICA

EUROPE

ASIA

AFRICA

SOUTH AMERICA

AUSTRALIA

Ecuador is a country in the **continent** of South America.

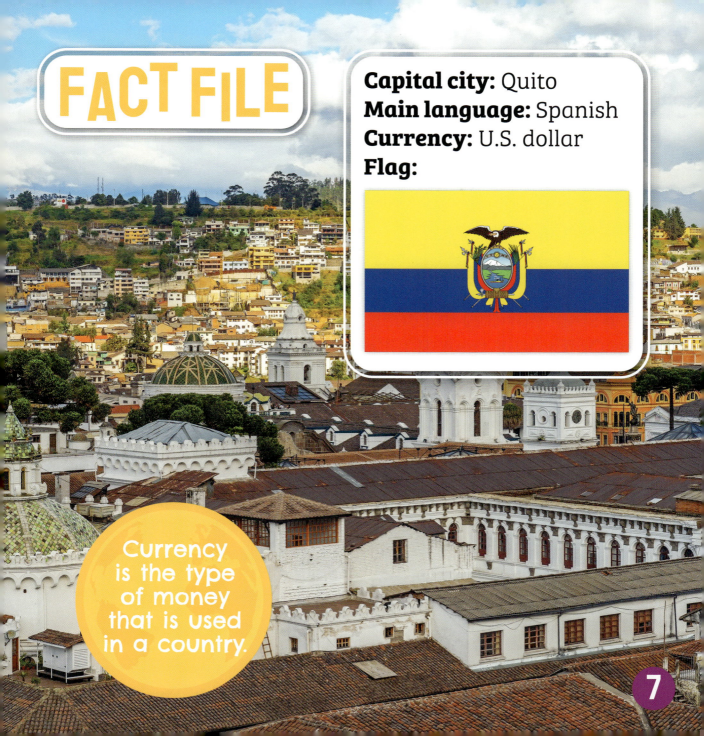

FACT FILE

Capital city: Quito
Main language: Spanish
Currency: U.S. dollar
Flag:

Currency is the type of money that is used in a country.

QUITO

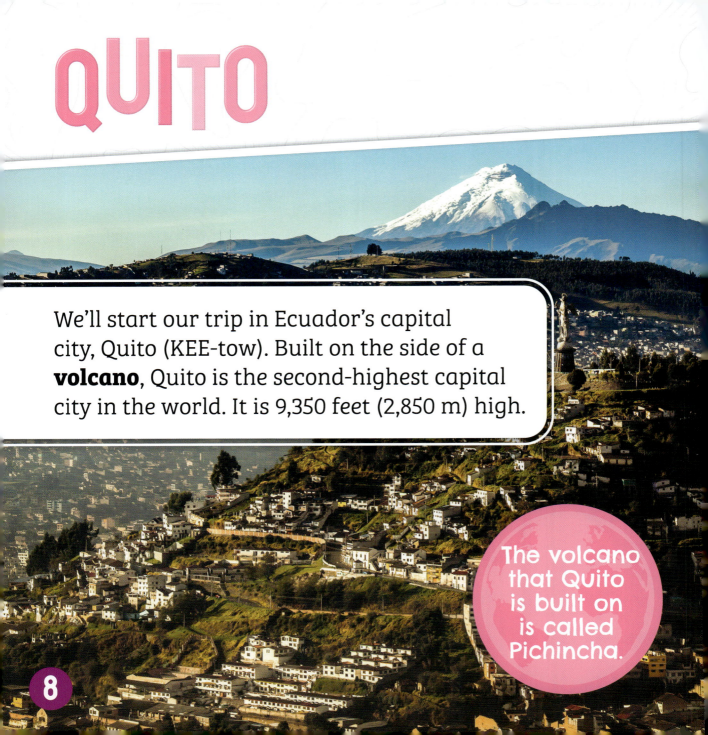

We'll start our trip in Ecuador's capital city, Quito (KEE-tow). Built on the side of a **volcano**, Quito is the second-highest capital city in the world. It is 9,350 feet (2,850 m) high.

The volcano that Quito is built on is called Pichincha.

There is an area of Quito called Old Town that has lots of very old buildings. Many people enjoy visiting this historic and beautiful part of the city.

VOLCANOES

Chimborazo has snow at its top.

The capital city is not the only place in Ecuador with volcanoes. The country has many, including Chimborazo. This large volcano is more than 20,000 ft (6,100 m) high.

One of Ecuador's islands has a volcano called Sierra Negra. At the top is a huge, round **crater** more than 5 miles (8 km) wide. It is the second-largest crater on Earth!

Sierra Negra crater

MINDO CLOUD FOREST

Next, let's visit the Mindo Cloud Forest. This mountain area is home to hundreds of different kinds of birds. Many of them have amazing, colorful beaks and feathers.

Plate-billed mountain toucan

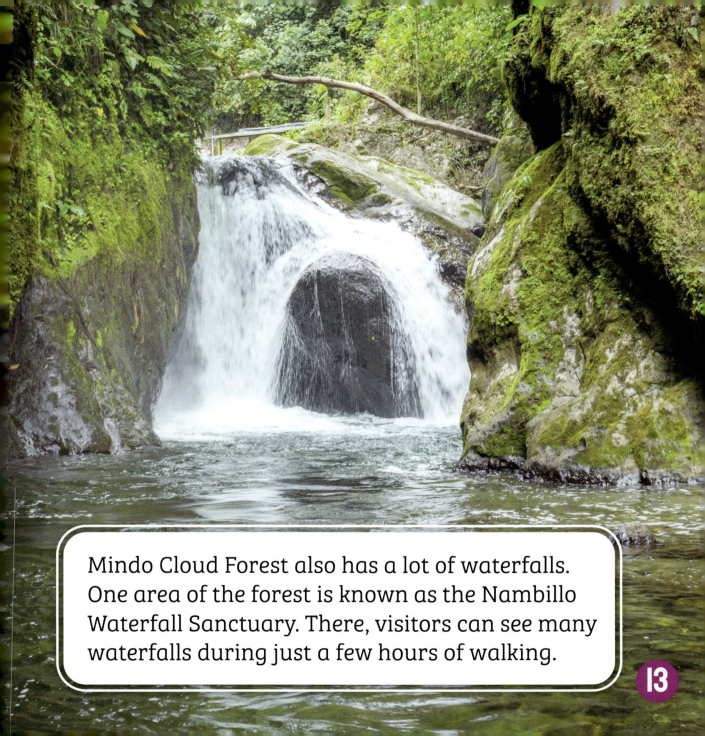

Mindo Cloud Forest also has a lot of waterfalls. One area of the forest is known as the Nambillo Waterfall Sanctuary. There, visitors can see many waterfalls during just a few hours of walking.

ANIMALS

Galápagos tortoise

Ecuador has a lot of animals that cannot be found anywhere else in the world. Some live in the Amazon rain forest. Others, such as giant Galápagos tortoises, live on Ecuador's Galápagos Islands.

Tapirs look a little bit like pigs with longer noses. But these animals from Ecuador are actually more closely related to horses and rhinos.

Tapir

OTAVALO

Let's go to the city of Otavalo, where we'll find one of the most famous markets in South America. At the Otavalo Market, Ecuador's Otavaleño people sell colorful hats, clothes, and pottery.

The Otavaleño people were among the first groups to live in Ecuador. They have a big **festival** in Otavalo every year to celebrate the corn they've grown. This festival is called Yamor.

FOOD

What can we eat in Ecuador? *Ceviche* is a popular dish made of shrimp or fish with onions, peppers, and a lime-flavored sauce.

For a treat, let's try *espumilla* (ESS-pooh-MEE-ya). This creamy, fruity dessert is often eaten from a cone. It looks like ice cream, but it doesn't melt in hot weather!

INGAPIRCA

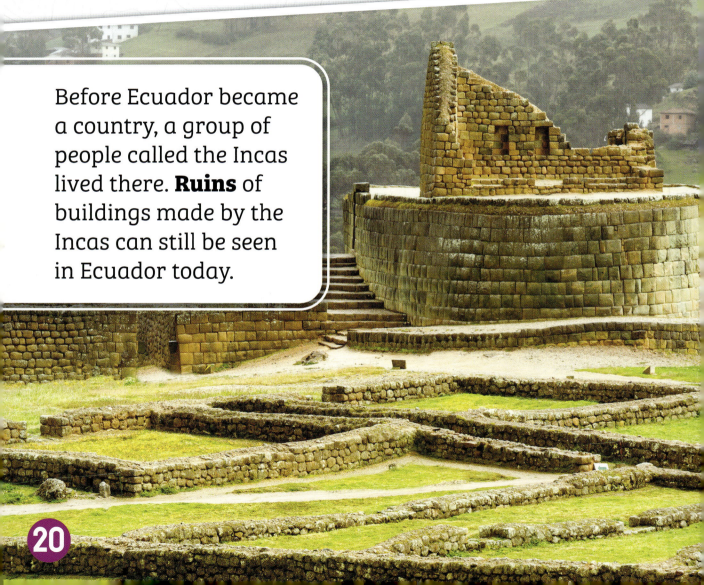

Before Ecuador became a country, a group of people called the Incas lived there. **Ruins** of buildings made by the Incas can still be seen in Ecuador today.

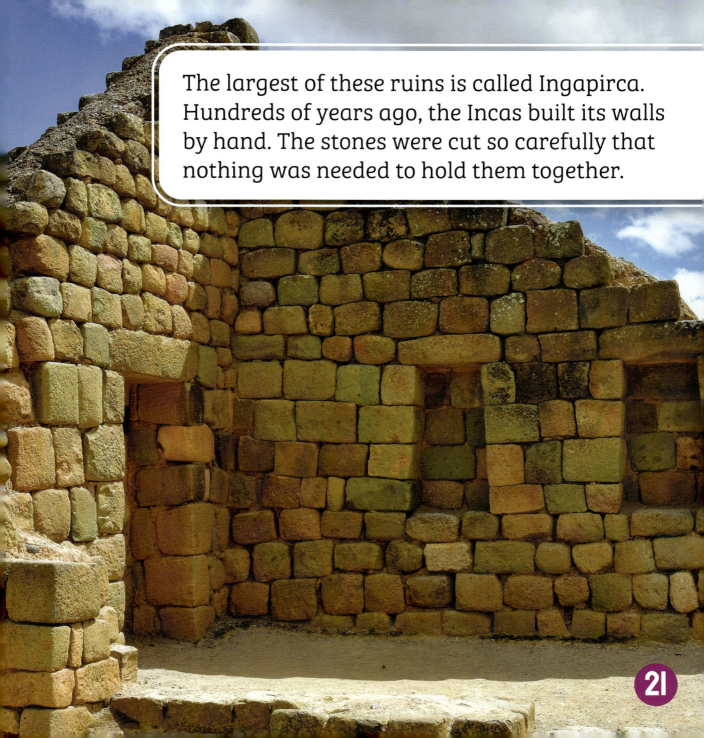

The largest of these ruins is called Ingapirca. Hundreds of years ago, the Incas built its walls by hand. The stones were cut so carefully that nothing was needed to hold them together.

BEFORE YOU GO

We can't forget to visit the city of Baños! There are lots of things to do there. Many visitors enjoy walking over the long bridge to see the nearby waterfall.

We could also take the Nariz del Diablo train ride, which goes up the edge of a steep hill. It zigzags back and forth past some amazing views on its way to the top.

What have you learned about Ecuador on this trip?

GLOSSARY

borders lines that show where one place ends and another begins

continent one of the world's seven large land masses

crater a large, shallow hole at the top of a volcano

festival an event for lots of people to come together and celebrate

ruins buildings that have been partly destroyed or broken down over time

volcano a mountain that can erupt to let out hot, melted rock

INDEX